Dorp Dea

At first Gilly Ground, a foxy but sensitive boy, is grateful to get away from the orphanage and go to live as apprentice to Mr. Kobalt, the ladder maker. But life in that strange stone house is as ordered and disquieting as a metronome's beat, and before long Gilly recognizes its sinister undercurrent. There is a blood-chilling confrontation before he and Mash, the sad dog he has befriended, can make their escape.

spanfeller

JULIA CUNNINGHAM

Dorp Dead

Illustrated by James Spanfeller

ALFRED A. KNOPF · NEW YORK

For Tuppy,
together with
love and honor,
violets and cyclamen

Originally published in New York by Pantheon Books, a division of Random House, Inc., and simultaneously in Toronto, Canada, by Random House of Canada Limited.
Manufactured in the United States of America
First Borzoi Sprinters 1987, Edition
2 4 6 8 10 9 7 5 3 1

Library of Congress Cataloging-in-Publication Data
Cunningham, Julia. Dorp {sic} dead.
Summary: When a lonely boy leaves an orphanage to be apprenticed to a laddermaker only to find out that he is a virtual prisoner, he seeks escape with the one affectionate creature in his life, the dog Mash. {1. Orphans—Fiction} I. Spanfeller, James J., 1930— , ill.
II. Title. III. Title: Dorp dead. PZ7.C9167Do 1987 {Fic} 87-3735
ISBN 0-394-91089-3 (lib. bdg.) ISBN 0-394-89267-4 (pbk.)

Dorp Dead

1

This is the account that was found after it was all over. The very confused spelling has been corrected out of respect for the young writer, Gilly Ground.

This story starts and middles and ends with me. I guess I was always what is called different, or way out, or a little nuts. Like me or not, that's how it is. Oh, I look like any other eleven-year-old with a thatch of roughly cut brown hair, the correct number of fingers and toes, green eyes that can open or shut with sun or sleep, and a sort of over-all foxy face, narrow at the chin. But I have a secret that nobody, not my dead grandmother or Mrs. Heister at the orphanage or my various unfortunate teachers, ever guessed. I am ferociously intelligent for my age and at ten I hide this. It is a weapon for defense as comforting as a very sharp knife worn between the skin and the shirt. When a person hasn't money in the pocket, good leather to walk around in, clothes that are his own, and a home address to back him up, I figure he has to have something else — anything. And I'm lucky. I'm not just bright, I'm brilliant, the way the sun is at noon. This is not a boast. It's the truth. It's my gold, my shelter, and my pride. It's completely my possession and I save it like an old miser to spend later. I purposely never learn to spell, which for the simple indicates stupidity. I fall all over my tongue when I am asked to read in school, and when we have a test in arithmetic I dig in the wrong answers very hard with a soft pencil and then smudge them over with my thumb to make it look as though I had tried.

I realize that I sound pretty unsavory, and maybe if my soft little grandmother had lived longer and I hadn't been thrown into the orphanage the day before I got to be ten I might have chosen to stand and shine. She would have been proud of me and that would have given me a reason. But she didn't and she died poor, so my story, as me, really starts over a year ago on a chill autumn night having a rather scrawny arm pinched by the thunderous Mrs. Heister, superintendent of the village Home for Children.

This big, overstuffed woman has nothing against me. She doesn't know me that well. But to her I am another bed, another hunger to feed, and maybe another contact for her switch, which in all justice to her, she only uses when forced to by a major rebellion. She tells me there are no rules except co-operation, obedience, and attention to homework and then calls in a senior citizen of about fifteen, who leads me off like a small dog to a long, windowed room, points at a cot with red blankets, says "That's yours," and takes off.

I see the other inmates are already settled on their pillows, though they are giving me the eye all the time I am undressing which is slightly embarrassing as my pajamas are colorfully patched from all views. One shrimpy guy across the aisle ventures a weak "Hello" and another voice from the corner region calls out, "You'll get used to it." But I reply to neither. I am alone and on my own since my grandmother has been tucked away forever, and I intend to stay that way. I bear no grudges toward the world. I just figure I've a lot to learn and to sort out after I've learned it and it will be easier if I don't get too tangled up with people, or at least, not until I'm better acquainted with how people are.

I insert myself between the covers and send a smile up to where my grandmother is — she always believed she was going to a better place where her house would have a kitchen as big as a barn, with tables and chairs and paintings of flowers on the walls, and if her new country is well organized, I'm certain she has all these things. This seems to warm the damp sheets and I fall into sleep like a ripe apple leaves the branch.

I wake up the next morning, as I will wake up all the next three hundred and sixty-five mornings until the changes come, to a series of bongs that bounce off my ear-drums and then ring an extra time in my skull. I shake my head like trying to get water out of the ears and look around. The rest of them are already up and out and racing for the bathrooms next door. I lie quiet for a couple of minutes, a habit I adopt then and for good, to let the first line-up thin out, then I shovel myself out of bed, walk to the nearest unoccupied basin, douse my pointy face once, draw a brush rapidly over my front teeth, take a couple of swipes at my hair, and return to my clothes, which are no problem, being so basic: underwear, shorts, tee shirt, and sweater. My socks and shoes take an extra thirty seconds, as I am inclined to get dreamy over putting them on. If I am ever rich — I assume a cynical grin at my own foolishness — I will use up at least ten minutes on socks. This is the time my best thinking is done, so why waste it?

I observe the next step is to make beds, so I stretch my blanket tight over the under-rumple of sheets, smooth my pillow, and then follow the other guys outdoors and into a low, one-story building that, on entering, smells of old grease and new bread. We line up and with a maximum of clatter each take a metal tray, dented by generations of orphans, and shuffle forward slowly to where the cook, a man as skinny as his soups, slaps a heavy bowl of oatmeal on each one, contributing another dent. Later I make an enemy of this man by being nervous and accidentally letting the bowl slide onto the floor. And oatmeal, when slushed under many feet, is no pleasure to scrub up. So from then on, after we have helped ourselves to three chunks of bread and one square of butter and he is now stationed at the end of the counter pitchering out milk, he fixes me with a ration of milk one inch short of the brim of the glass. He also looks as if he'd like to plop a cockroach into the liquid, but never does. I rule him out as a person after this, though I've peeled many a peck of potatoes in his dour company.

After breakfast we get ten minutes to ourselves and then we are ticked off for Special Duties: sweeping, washing dishes from yesterday, shelving groceries, chopping wood for the three fireplaces, and all the other jobs needed to keep extreme dilapidation from becoming ruins.

I wasn't too bored by a series of experiments at washing dishes without soap until Mrs. Heister, on her daily Reviewing the Troops Inspection, caught me out, at which point I was put on the woodpile for two weeks. But mostly I just slog through without much conversation with my fellow workers, an attitude that crowns me with the nickname "Snobby Gilly." I don't mind this at all. It gives me privacy.

Next we have exercises and I wise up very soon that the last line is the best. Here I can bounce to the rhythms, fling my arms skyward when the other arms are doing the same, and generally not strain myself. These back-border positions are very popular and a couple of times I have to fight to keep mine, but I'm pretty tough in the muscles, thanks to having pushed a few thousand cartfuls of laundry up and down the streets of the village for my grandmother and sometimes helping her with the heavy ironing nights when her back ached so badly I'd catch tears in her eyes.

Then, from nine to one, school. There isn't much more to report about these long, stringy mornings, at least not my part in them, which, as I have mentioned earlier, is mostly taken up with stuttering through the readers, smearing tests with wrong answers, and gazing blank-eyed out of the windows, all so as to cement the impression that I'm stupid.

I glide through the boredom of these mornings with tolerance toward all except one thing — the terrible bonging bells that Mrs. Heister's got a passion for. Sometimes

I try to create enough silence in my head so I can fold myself up in it as in a giant quilt, but this never really works. The whole day, from the bell that shocks me out of bed, that begins the continuous noise of the other guys talking and yelling, until the final whispering from bed to bed at night, seems like one huge tumult to my insides and sometimes I wish so fiercely to be free of it that I discover my teeth are grinding together like two sets of electric saws.

But there is a good hour. It arrives after lunch-with-leftovers, after the following study hall. We are instructed in this free period to go no farther than the village and back, but I know a place on a mountain I can get to, if I run both ways, where quiet lives and makes me welcome. There, in the center of a tall stand of pines, is a very ancient, very crumbly ruin of a tower. There are no signs or marks to tell its age and it is open to the sky. It has only five high steps inside that once wound to the top, and until I cleaned it up it was crammed with rubble and fallen fragments of its own stones. Nobody comes but me because the pathway is now so thick with thorn bushes and underbrush it's more like a tunnel than a trail, and this is my kingdom and my home. I see nobody. Well, it was nobody until one strange day when I was already eleven and the Hunter appeared. But I'm leapfrogging ahead of what happened.

In these days of my being ten, I sit on the small throne

I construct by stacking four squared stones in the shape of one and gaze out through a jagged gap into a distance of river and hills and changing clouds, and let the peace gather itself up in me like the bunches of wild violets and cyclamen I used to pick for my grandmother on Sundays. Sometimes I am late getting back to the misery of the bells and Mrs. Heister sets me to weeding crabgrass with a rusty trowel that leaves stains like blood on my fingers. She never knows I rather take to this punishment because I am always careful to look sullen when she thrusts the trowel at me. I pretend the stubborn underground streamers are enemies and root up their tough, resisting menace like a knight unhorsing his foes, one by one, at some glittering, bannered tournament.

Then the bell bongs for recreation. This hour and a half before supper usually signals my limit for the absorption of clamor, so once the teams are chosen and the game begins, I stuff two grubby wads of cotton in my ears and watch the ball. But because I am blocked off from warning shouts and orders, I often louse up several plays before I am kicked off the field and at liberty to stow away in the tool shed at the edge of the yard until the next crashing of the gong, which means wash hands for dinner. Anyone can see why I am never very popular or sought after: a stuffed bear in school, from whom infrequent and inaccurate grunts of non-knowledge are extracted, and a true clunk at sports, besides offering nothing in the way of malice or inventiveness in between. This is the way I want it and have it.

After the repeat of the clattery trays, the grub, which is never uneatable just all the time watery, and the last study hall, we are bonged to bed and the day ends in a couple of mild pillow fights, underbreath conferences, and small tussles, none of which I join, and after a grateful while of silence, I sleep.

So go my days for that grey and gritty year when I move one step forward from being ten to being eleven, and it is right after a birthday no one but me remembers that the first tremors of the craziness vibrate under my running feet.

2

This particular morning there is nothing special about the sky. It is overweighed with soiled clouds, but it often is when the year revolves slowly toward winter. I am awake and open-eyed enough to look up and down the rows of beds, each.loaded with a sleeper. This, too, is like yesterday and the day before and all the days backward. I am tensing my body against the shatterment of the first gong and this also is a daily habit. But something, I don't know what, is different inside me, sort of as though I, too, am heading toward winter, toward becoming very gradually iced all over whether I will it or not. Maybe it is being newly eleven, but I get no echo of reassurance from this conclusion so I decide it must be something else that is sending little rills of shivers up and down my backbone.

Then that first awful bell explodes in the room and I explode with it. I scrabble into my clothes, ignore the yells of astonishment as I race past the bathrooms and into the yard, slamming the door behind me with a crash like forever. I dive into the rear entrance of the kitchen, grab up a small loaf of bread and dig into the vegetable bin, coming up with three carrots, and then scuttle out just as the cook appears, his slack and startled mouth practically showing his tonsils.

I hardly know what I am doing or why but I have to get out, all the way out, and I find my legs taking me in a long, striding rush into the thickets and up the mountain.

Not until I am seated for five minutes on my king's chair does the pounding in my chest slacken and my throat feel less like a sand pit. I don't try to think or wonder about why I am here so fast, so urgently. I just stay on that hollowed stone, relaxed and, at least for now, rooted. I close my eyes and am listening to the stillness of the pines and peaks when, very faintly, a small and distant *crack-crackle* as of disturbed twigs begins to near my tower. I am about to believe it is a bear or a stray goat when suddenly, blanking out three-quarters of the arched door-hole, I see the silhouette of a man entirely clothed in black.

For some reason I get to my feet. I wait.

He enters and now the sunlight from the window-slit shows a long narrow face with deep-lidded eyes and a sober mouth. He is looking at me as though I were not a surprise but an intruder. This jerks me out of my stiffness. It is my tower.

"Who are you?" I ask evenly. I want no enemies but I also want no friends. Not here in my secret property.

"I am a hunter," he answers as though a name is of no importance.

For the first time I notice the gun held loosely in his right hand, a hand that matches his face for length.

He moves over to my window and gazes out at my mountains and my sky.

"What do you hunt?" I want to fill the tower with questions that will make him wish to leave.

He stays motionless, his back to me. "Nothing. I hunt to see. My gun carries no bullets."

"Then why a gun at all?"

Now he is facing me, and for an instant his mouth is brushed by a smile. "For protection." He tranquilly sits down on my throne but I do not tell him to get up. He seems to belong to it in a weird sort of way, as though he were no stranger to majesty, even as crude a kind as this.

I pause to find out if he has anything to ask me, but

there is no sound in the tower except the tiny ruffles of wind that lick gently at the crumbled edges of the entryway. There is no awkwardness in or around him and not the slightest stir in his body. He is planted and peaceful, enthroned there on my chair, and the tower seems his instead of mine but somehow I do not resent it. I am the one who is restless. I remember my loaf of bread and three carrots. The thought strikes me as a little crazy but I wish I had a plate to put them on and a knife, both silver, before I say, "Would you like some lunch?"

He gives my sorry feast his full attention and there is no smile this time, just a small inclination of his dark head as he replies, "No, but I thank you." My offer of refreshments seems to have loosened his formality. He asks, "Where do you live, boy?"

"In the town orphanage," I reply.

"I, too, grew up alone," he says, and now his tallness is less tall.

"Oh, I do okay," I comment, never having been one who mouses around for sympathy. "I had a first-class grandmother until last year. Then she died."

"I'm sorry." And he really sounds it.

"Well, she was tired and now she isn't any more, so I guess I shouldn't complain. Except that I miss her."

"You were fortunate." He is leaning forward a little, his hands resting on his knees.

"Yes, sir. I know that."

"You are how old? Ten?"

"Just past. Day before yesterday. I'm eleven now."

"Have you any plans? For later on?"

I wonder why this interest in puny old me. Is he kind, or merely filling in a morning with a stranger? I settle for the kindness theory because I'm pretty sure by this time that he never knew his grandmother or anyone else, at least not the way I did, someone who opened the door for him in the evening and had kisses to spare when the darkness came.

I half-smile at his question about plans. "Not likely. You aren't released from the Home until you are sixteen, and then the career of an orphan is up to him, assuming he's got the guts to go after one."

"And have you got the courage to?"

I am finding it very easy to talk to this man and I pretend for one luxurious moment that he is my father. I indulge in pure honesty. "I don't know yet. I have five years to go. But I hope I have."

He nods and I get the curious impression that he hopes so too. The Hunter — that is the name he has taken in my mind — rises. He doesn't simply leave the throne; he rises from it. He walks slowly to the doorway. "I must go on now. Towers like this are for one person, not two." He half-turns, once more blocking the clear and dustless sunlight. With a courtesy that reminds me of those hours in the tool shed when I swallowed a book about King

Arthur whole in one gulp of reading, he adds, "Good-bye."

"Will I see you again?" I ask. I realize I could learn to miss this mystery of a man.

"Perhaps," I hear coming from the path outside as he disappears down the first curve of the mountain.

I shrug. A perhaps is as good as a no in my language. I break off a chunk of bread and fill my mouth with it, and as I chew I taste none of the sweet saltiness of the loaf because I am thinking that the Hunter is like an eagle whose wingspread shadows the eyes for a moment and then vanishes forever. He does not fly the same way twice. I bite into a crisp carrot and crunch at it as if I were trying to shred the idea of the eagle into irretrievable splinters.

I spend the next couple of hours trying to fit some of the missing pieces and slabs of stone into the gaps of my tower. Without cement this is a matter of eye and balance, and when I take a break I accidentally go to sleep. I wake up into evening. All the way down the mountain I am puzzling as to why they didn't send out a search party for me. I've been gone an entire day, which makes me a major truant, and I can't remember when this ever happened before at the orphanage.

But the minute I walk into the yard I know why. Mrs. Heister is stationed stock in the center of everything, swaying a little from side to side as though she has been

on her feet for quite a while. Her hands go on her hips when she spies me coming and her voice is loud. "You may come in by the front door, young man, as a visitor." She swivels about-face and marches back into the building.

While I am skirting the side lawn I feel goosebumps prickling my arms. The woman is really angry. I hesitate at the blank solidity of the door and note that my hand is somewhat shaky as I raise it to knock. One tap and the door is open with Mrs. Heister on the other side larger than life-size, her face as red as beet juice.

"Come in." I follow her into her study. "Sit down." She points to a straight brown chair and I sit in it. She remains standing, so close she sort of looms. "Gillford Ground, you are a real disturbance to us all. You apply yourself to nothing, not to your schoolwork, to your chores, or to the friendliness of your companions. In short, you do not fit in here and it has been your own choice not to do so." She halts here to take a breath or maybe because she doesn't want to say what comes next. She's not a mean woman, just limited. I have thoughts about solitary confinement, a diet of bread and water, and even a beating, though that is seldom practiced in this institution. But the words that come from her are none of these and I am almost jolted off my seat. "I have found you a foster home." She lets this sink in and it does. Who in the village would be willing to take in the most undesirable orphan in the Home? The other kids talk continually about how they would give anything for the chance to be in a house private to them, and how it would be to maybe have a room with one bed in it, their own, instead of twenty. But they know they are too old to be trusted and wanted, that they have lived too long on the outside. So now, why me?

She seems to guess what whirls around in my head. "This will not be an easy placement. For you," she adds separately for emphasis.

"Who is it?" I burst through.

"Mr. Kobalt."

Kobalt, the ladder maker! The town eccentric. The man who never speaks to anyone except the grocer and his own mud-colored dog. I remember a town kid telling me once about how they don't even dare call names after him in the street. And when I asked why, the boy just answered, "You wouldn't either." But he's said to be rich. He has the only stone house in the village and all the ladders he carpenters are sold in the city, fifty miles away, at a special shop. Why Kobalt?

"When am I going?" I begin to warm up inside. I'm getting a prize position. But why?

"At seven-thirty tomorrow morning. I will see that you are ready. Mr. Kobalt only comes out of his house three times a day and one of those times is at eight, to let out his dog. He will receive you then. And one more thing. If you fail to satisfy you will be sent to an orphanage in the city, a very different sort of place from this. So be forewarned." She looms a bit nearer as if her body could drive in the solemnity of her advice. Then she moves off. "Good night, Gillford," and she waits for me to leave. I do and all the way back and into my bed I am suspended between the jitters and a thin rope of something like hope. Maybe, I think as I draw the sheet up and over my blanket and fasten it with my chin, all the wrinkles of noise and confusion, all the angular corners of my days in the orphanage will smooth out flat in the house of grey stone with the crystal-clean windows. Or, I think again, as my two big toes begin to curl in involuntary cramps, maybe not.

3

I am awake and ready when the morning gong lets out its howl and am buttoning my jacket with rather numb fingers when Mrs. Heister beckons at the door for me to accompany her to the kitchen. There the cook, looking less like a raddled cucumber, no doubt because this is my last day, hands me a tray with the usual oatmeal, bread, and a Sunday egg, though this is Wednesday. I sit beside Mrs. Heister, the two of us at a table for twenty, and find it difficult to eat without the usual tumble of talk and squeals and shin-kicking. We have no conversation.

At last we get up, she heaves into her coat, and we start for the village. She has to deliver me but I get the feeling, as we walk down the dirt road of the orphanage and arrive at the cobbled outskirts of the town, that she isn't liking it much. Not because she is fond of me. She hasn't time for attachment to anybody. But maybe because I am one of her failures. She even notices I am a bit shivery under the weakness of the sun and the cut of the early air and pulls my coat collar up against the back of my neck. This reminds me of my grandmother and I indulge in the hopeless wish that she were with me instead, smelling as she always did of fresh-mown alfalfa. I realize I must toughen these few last soft spots in my character, and I straighten my shoulders as we tramp down the main street, past the shuttered stores and two-story houses. A little girl waves to me from a doorstep and a sparrow squeaks a "Good morning" from one of the trees that form a double lane down the center of the street, but I respond to neither. I want no involvements, not in the orphanage and not here in the village, and that includes sparrows as well as people.

Finally we stop before the grey house, so perfectly square of shape and so immaculate it looks as if someone scrubs it every day. I am surprised that Mrs. Heister doesn't knock. She simply stands there in front of the varnished door. But we do not wait long. Thirty seconds later it opens and the space is filled by the width of a man so muscled his grey suit must be made to order to fit him. And he is not much over five feet high. He merely nods at Mrs. Heister and then lets his eyes rove all over me as though he were outlining every detail of my small shabbiness on paper with a fine-point pen. I stay very still until he is finished.

He says "Goodbye" to Mrs. Heister, then turns sideways in the doorway and I realize I am supposed to go in. I put out my hand to the woman who has bedded and fed me for more than a year. She takes it but our fingers touch rather than clasp, and she says something about my behaving myself and goes off toward the market place. I inhale a last lungful of the outer world, step inside, and then let out my breath so fast it clouds the air. I am in the middle of a little palace! But before I have the chance to do more than get a fuzzed impression of the polished wood and velvet and the sculptured fireplace, the man speaks and I have to strain a little to catch the low, cello-pitched words. "When you address me, and let this be only when strictly necessary, you will call me Master Kobalt. I shall give you, this first day, one hour to know my house. I live in lanes of time; each hour is channeled. You will fit into these grooves. Your job will be to plane the wood I use for my ladders but you are never to touch any part of my work or tools. I am now going to buy the day's food and will return at the end of your hour."

I murmur, "Yes, sir," and he treads the floor so heavily

going to the door that I can feel the vibrations even under the thick carpeting.

"It is quiet here," he adds as he starts to shut the door on himself. "I wish it so." The door clicks shut and I hear a key lock it tight. I wonder why but only until I inspect the double-plated glass windows and see that they, too, are fastened, with tiny padlocks.

I start to grin. Well, if I am a prisoner, at least I am a royal one.

This is a house like a very detailed drawing that someone has sketched and resketched, placed and replaced for hundreds of evenings until it is, down to the box of matches on the exact center of the mantel, perfect. And there is a feeling in the exactitude of every table, chair, picture, and kitchen canister, that no carelessness or rearrangement will ever be permitted. And it strikes me, though my experience only takes in my grandmother's one-chair, one-bed, one-plate-apiece kind of interior, that Master Kobalt has not created this shiny, absolute precision out of love but because it creates safety for him. I sound profound. I'm not. It just comes to me on account of how I feel about my drafty, unfurnished tower. I understand the need, and Kobalt, unlike me, has the means to fix it this way.

And another thing. As I stroll through the square living room where the six cushioned, gilt-legged chairs all face the wood-readied fireplace and the faces of the single portraits, one on each wall, are hung to look into their opposites' eyes, I find myself not only understanding but approving. This is manufactured peace, but it's peace and I like it. I turn left from the living room across a narrow hall that contains a staircase and into such a kitchen I burst out laughing and almost hear my grandmother laugh with me. Its canary-yellow walls, waxed counters, black tiled stove, three-tiered cupboards, round table, and three chairs are so clean, so speckless, one couldn't imagine so much as a fly entering this room without collapsing. I even worry that the soles of my rotting shoes may leave permanent stains on the grey stone floor. The room looks as though it has never been cooked in. The only oddment in it is a cage made of thin plywood slats. It looks like something a cat or dog lives in, and though there is an entrance slot, there is no door to fit it.

The only other room off the hall, toward the back, is Kobalt's workshop. It is as big as the living room and kitchen combined, lined with benches where rows of tools glimmer in their straightness like regiments of toy soldiers. The fifteen saws — I count them — might have been bought yesterday; their teeth are wiped utterly free of sawdust, their handles undulled by fingerprints or dried sweat. Then I realize why my nose is sniffing the air with such pleasure. The wood, the three tall stacks of rough, sweet-smelling lumber. In one corner is a neat pile of unfinished rungs, in another the side rails.

I close the door quickly as I leave, so as not to dissipate the fragrance.

Next I go upstairs. There are only three doors off the tiny corridor. The first is locked. This must be Kobalt's room. The second is a bathroom. The third I enter. I know immediately that it is mine. The bed is better than a cot, already high with covers tucked in triangularly at the corners. A plain, oblong table with one center drawer, faced by a straight chair, has a midnight-blue blotter cut exactly to its size and a pen and pencil aligned across the top. I peek into the closet. My breath cuts short. There hang a bear-brown coat of thick wool with a belt and a pair of winter trousers, and two pairs of shoes, one for outdoors with laces, the other of felt with pliable leather soles, are placed neatly side by side on the closet floor. And they are all my size! My breathing still captured, I cautiously slide out the two drawers of the floor chest beside the bed and there, lying ironed and new, are three blue shirts, three pairs of wool socks, two sets of underwear, and five cotton handkerchiefs. My size again, except for the handkerchiefs that would serve anyone's nose. I suddenly get a rush of gratitude to the eyes and I pick up one of the handkerchiefs and use it. Then I hurry downstairs, return with my cardboard suitcase, empty it of my schoolbooks, which is all it contains except a little tin-framed snapshot I have of my grandmother taken at a county fair when she was younger than I remember her, and I arrange the books in a geometric pattern on the blotter. For some strange reason my grandmother's picture doesn't seem to go anyplace, though I try it on each wall. It puts the room off balance. So, not letting any thoughts form on the subject, I hurriedly shove it under my shirts and close the drawer.

My hour must be about up so I start down the stairs, touching the satiny banister with my forefinger all the way to the bottom, and stand motionless in the hall listening to the silence that is measured only by the one item I left out — the five clocks in each of the rooms downstairs.

I'm not alone long. The fifteen clocks are just beginning their nine concerted strokes, all of them with voices no more strenuous than a titmouse's cheep, when a key clicks back the lock in the front door and in steps Mr. Kobalt. He nods as though we had greeted each other every morning for ten years, hands me the string bag bulgy with groceries, and I follow him into the kitchen. He points to the cupboards and I understand I am to put everything away. But what has startled me into such temporary awkwardness I drop a can of beans, is the dog who sits on the threshold and watches us.

Kobalt rubs the toe of his shoe over the scratch the fallen can has marked on the floor and is about to take off when I stop him with, "Thank you very much, sir, for the clothes. It's the first time in my life I ever had anything new and —— "

"You shall be properly dressed in my house," he cuts in, canceling the thanks or any repetition of them in tones so positive I couldn't miss the point if I were as dense as a deaf pig. "To cut down the questions I will tell you your duties during lunch, which is at twelve noon. I assemble this meal. You the supper. I am going to my workshop and will emerge at eleven-thirty." His broad back is to me now and he is on his way. As he passes through the hall I hear his last, low, penetrating words: "The dog's name is Mash."

It takes me a half-hour to stow the food and memorize the cupboards, where the cleaning rags and liquids and powders are ranged by size, the smaller citizens to the fore; the vegetable bins, all labeled — *Onions, Carrots, Beans, Potatoes, Turnips*; the meat cooler; the bread box; the drawers with their knives and spoons and forks, each slotted and ready for use. This is as different from the muddled, bent, and haphazard equipment of the orphanage as a straight wire is from a twisted.

I figure I am now at liberty to make friends with the dog, and such an animal I have never seen before in street or alley. His coat of short hairs is so clean it gleams, or would if his color weren't so completely drab. It actually isn't a color but is as though someone had achieved the muddiest mudpie in the world and then painted this bony creature all over with it and I mean all over. Even the dog's eyes give no relief, being a sort of yellowish,

weathered brown like his fur. His lank ears hang like flaps, his tail is a mere end of rope, stumped off at the end about a foot from his rear, and his paws are like blobs tied onto his stringy legs at the last minute. I don't like or dislike him. He is inferior and he knows it. I pat the top of his knobby head and he just squats there, blinking at me out of his round, expressionless eyes.

I try talking. "Hello, old Mash, how goes it? Want a scratch behind the ears? Like this?" There is no response. I might as well be chatting with a tree stump. I rub my hand down his ridged back. I am interested because I am curious. He is built skinny, a skin stuffed with sticks, but he's not hungry. He has his place in this warmth and comfort. He hasn't been beaten. His body is sleek and cared-for. Then why does he seem so absent from his own carcass? Where and why is he hiding? I decide to treat him with honor. This works sometimes with orphans. I've seen it happen. They get to believe they are somebody better than just themselves. I begin small. I get up off my own haunches and start trotting around the circular table. "Come on, Mash, catch me!"

He cocks his head but doesn't move. Well, this is a kind of progress. At least I get him to wondering who the dickens this new character is who whips around tables going nowhere.

Soon I sit down myself, on one of the three chairs, and

let the strengthening heat of the sun that squares me off from the window like a portrait seep into my skin and even past the peaky bones of my face until my thoughts become dreams and my eyelids drift shut.

4

I settle into the routine of Kobalt's life as smoothly as if a mold has been devised just my size and all I have to do is to fit myself into it, which I do from that very first day. Mostly I appreciate the intense quiet that begins at seven when I slow-motion out of bed into my new clothes and go down to my small jobs in the kitchen. I put water on to boil, get the eggs out of the cooler, slice the bread, two for each, set the table, and generally organize the breakfast.

My patron stumps in at seven-thirty. I say, "Good morning, Master Kobalt," and he replies simply, "Good morning," never using my name, which I stop wondering about after the third or fourth time. He also never looks directly at me, or if he does when his massive head is bent downward I wouldn't know it, his eyebrows being like awnings over his eye sockets. We eat without any chat whatsoever and then I wash the couple of plates and cups while he gets his market basket set up. At the exact melodious strikes of the fifteen clocks, five for each room as I mentioned before, he is out of the front door and on his way while I let Mash out of the workroom and take him around to the tiny garden in back with its patch of grass bordered by rosebushes as high as my head and tie the end of his long rope-lead to the doorknob of the tool shed.

We have a small conversation, with me telling him how much I approve of his peculiar baked-mud color, his lop ears and his lumpy shape, and after the third morning I get a tail wag that on any other dog would mean the wind pushed at it slightly but that for Mash may be the first stir of friendship. The wag becomes wider as the days add up to more talks, but I'm not hoping to ever be a witness to a genuine sweep of his wandlike extremity.

Then I report myself to the carpenter shop where I place the first plank of the dozens Kobalt has piled up for me into a vise and plane it so fine my thumbs can waltz all over it without encountering a thread of a splinter. I enjoy this backward and forward rhythm, as if my arm and hand are skating on glass, and when Kobalt enters at nine to the second to take up his more complicated actions of beveling and fitting and waxing I am already half-hypnotized by the quiet, the silent slide of my tool, and the ripe fragrance of the wood. At eleven-thirty Kobalt exits to prepare the lunch and I stack my finished planks and take up the broom to rid the entire room of shavings and sawdust.

At twelve the clocks tell me to join him in the kitchen where several mounds of good meat and vegetables are already steaming on my large plate. I wash and sit down to it with an occasional remembering of my grandmother who mostly filled herself and me up with potatoes, and I eat the dish empty. Mash watches us from inside his open cage.

By the time I restore the kitchen to its usual neat shine it is one o'clock, and my school hours take me to four in the afternoon. It's plenty odd about me and school now. I check in once a week with the village teacher for my lessons and to hand over test papers and get the same back, but I do all my scholarly headwork by myself. Kobalt has accomplished this arrangement and it will continue until my card begins to sprout E's and F's, which it doesn't. I earn the top of the alphabet in every subject except spelling. I try to dope out why I refuse to keep in mind that "rabbit" has two *b's* and one *t* and all I come up with is that a person has to hold out against being the same as everyone else, even if only over a few words like rabbit. A guy I knew by sight at the orphanage wore his button-down sweater backwards and this interested me until I asked him one day why and he said he'd always wanted a pullover so this was second best. My hopes for him vanished. He wouldn't have understood my necessity to jumble letters.

Anyway, to get on with it, I'm commencing to worry that I'll soon be labeled the brightest student in the one-room schoolhouse, so infrequently I mess up a history exam or shove Italy over next to India and these tricks appear to satisfy the teacher that I continue to be erratic. I find my schoolbooks somewhat elementary but I like to attach my elbows to my long desk in my room and let my mind drink up facts, all the while aware of the gone bongs of Mrs. Heister's institution and the vanished spitballs and scuffles of her study hours. I'm closed off and tight fitted within the four walls and I relish it.

At the next murmuring of the clocks I report to the broom closet in the front hall, extract the mop, broom, dustcloths, and pail, and burnish the house, all except Kobalt's room, which stays a mystery behind its locked door. I'm quite skilled, having learned on the floors and furniture of the orphanage. But here it is different. There is something vital about the order, the meticulous replacement of the squashy red rug in the living room after I've polished the dark hardwood under it, the resetting of the bowls in their special cupboards, the plumping-up of the hillocks of the chair cushions, even the removal of the dust particles from the underside of the stairway banister. I am not wholly alive to the importance of it until one afternoon when Mash accidentally joggles one of the three spindly tables in the living room and the china lamp on top of it teeters to the floor, cracking its parchment shade. Kobalt cancels the dog's meal that day, orders him into his box, and repairs the lamp, but the crack draws my look each time I enter the room instead of becoming a part of it. It is an imperfection in the absolute rightness of the rest.

Maybe I'm getting as queer as Kobalt but I don't worry because it agrees with me. Well, not entirely. I forget the hour between five and six, after I have put the evening soup on the stove to simmer, when I am free to go where I wish. The first few days I take myself for walks, usually to the village, and get acquainted with what's in the shop windows, who's treating whom to coffee and cakes in the town bakery — I don't go in but the whole front is glass — and a couple of times I even wander into the town hall, which is no bigger than the carpenter's house, and listen to the officials dealing with the citizens. This proves pretty dull, and besides, they quite obviously don't welcome the company of curious boys.

To get back to whether or not I'm becoming a character as fruity as Kobalt, it is hinted at the third day of my explorations of the village. A gaggle of boys and girls ranging around my age, but much more primary in their ideas, surround me and start a chant that makes me want to run. It goes: "Silly Gilly, Kobalt's goblin! Willy-nilly, he'll come soblin'!" Whatever my impulse I stand my foothold of ground and glare back at them until finally their voices dwindle down to stammers and they fling a few wildly aimed pebbles of gravel at me and take off. But I'm not too happy about this rhyme and I don't much want to hear it again, so after that I mostly use my free hour to sit in the tiny rose garden with Mash and read a book or gaze at clouds when there are enough to form imaginable shapes.

I go in at six, not even needing the clocks to summon me since my sense of time has sharpened considerably, and set the table while Kobalt ladles out the soup and cuts the bread. We eat. I stack the plates and bowls in the sink and then join the ladder maker in the living room where he is already reading his one book, a fat volume entitled *Time Patterns and How to Control Them*. He keeps his nose fastened to the pages for an hour and a half and then with a grunted "Good night" takes himself upstairs and locks himself in for the night. I get off my chair and lie before the dying kingdom of ember and ash, volcanoes and cindery plains, and sometimes the gentle warmth of the fire on my cheeks recalls the two kisses my dead grandmother used to plant on each side of my face every evening before she gave the covers a last tuck-in around my neck, and because she isn't with me any more, I put my hand on Mash's knobby head and stroke him between the ears. He grows to count on this, just as, long ago, I guess I counted on my grandmother to end the day sweetly.

Then I give him a final pat and mount the stairs to sleep.

5

So go my days for I forget how many weeks, maybe three or four, until one morning at seven I take a quick glance at myself in the bathroom mirror and am so startled I take another. My eyes look back at each other all blurry. Their color is green, an unsparkly kind at best, but it isn't just their dullness that shakes me. My face has lost its foxiness. Its edges are blunted and my cheeks seem a bit jowly. I blink for a couple of seconds. Maybe I just tunneled too deeply into night.

I scrub at my face and brush at my teeth with double energy, as though to scrape the mold from my mind. It isn't until I am downstairs and gulping at my oatmeal that I begin to jeer at myself for a fool. But all during the day the peace I get from planing lumber, from being holed up in my own room with my schoolbooks, from allowing the underwater plink-plunks of the fifteen clocks to measure my comings and goings, is pared off, as surely as the skin from an apple, and at five I do not take my usual route to the garden. I feel too crowded with lumps inside myself. Instead I get into my coat and hurry out into the street. I never question my direction. I am heading for the mountain.

I wonder as I go, for something to think about, why the path seems more choked with underbrush, why the tilt of the trail seems steeper, and why the tower, when at last it rises into sight, seems taller. I don't know why I have come here but when I reach the entrance I wish I were back behind the smooth stones of Kobalt's house. The round and rugged enclosure is occupied. There, standing tall and dark, is the Hunter.

He gazes at me all over as if I am some kind of being not yet catalogued. Then he recalls me completely and speaks: "You have been absent from your tower."

I nod. I have no reasons ready and am reluctant to dredge for any.

I begin to come alive. Why should this stranger of one long-ago morning care whether I come or not? What business is it of his? He has no claim on me. I remember vaguely how like a king he once was, seated on the throne that now looks like a careless tumble of giant rocks, but I toss out the image.

"I have missed you." He says this with such sincereness that I have to shove the words away from me, as I would his hand had he touched me.

I let a silence happen between us and strain to make it hostile, but am not succeeding very well because the next thing he says is, "Have you found another home?"

I leap into the gap he has shown me and I start to describe the beauty and serenity of my tower of hours in the house of the carpenter. At first my words come forth all haltered and abrupt and it is three minutes before I can recapture the normal rise and fall of a whole sentence. I guess it results from not speaking much any more except to Mash, and he can't answer back, which keeps our talks from becoming conversations.

But gradually, I hear myself filling the chill air with a fullness of how it is to have clothes worn only by me, of the three flavorsome meals, of my preparation of the rough wood that will be changed into strong and slender ladders, of my lazy hour in the garden and the final closing of the day within the glow of the expiring fire. I am certain of myself again and can dismiss the message of the mirror as an overdose of imagination.

I don't realize how far my tongue has journeyed until it stops, but the Hunter's attention is as focused as from the first phrase. There is a slight frown on his high forehead and his mouth is smiling at one corner, giving his narrow face a cast of something like the tenderness my grandmother's had when she had to scold me and didn't want to.

I wait, alert and sure, to defend myself against whatever comes out of him.

"Are you bewitched, boy?" he asks.

That's when such a gush of anger pushes at my throat I almost gag. I lose my head completely. "You're no better than the village gang, always jibbering rhymes at me about being Kobalt's goblin and such junk! What right have you to tell me how to run my life or to make fun of the only person in the world who would take in an orphan from a lousy institution where the noise is so crazy awful you wish you were born deaf? Who are you anyway, going around like a nut with an unloaded gun and no name, acting like the ruler of all the earth, interfering with people like me?" I am shouting now and want desperately to butt him full force in the stomach with my doubled fists.

He lets the flood of words and rage swirl around him until they are just eddies at his feet that finally drain off and out of the tower. He says nothing, but with motions as quiet as Mash's footpads on the carpet, he draws from his coat pocket a gold pen and a little red leather notebook. He writes on a page, tears it out, extracts a small envelope, inserts the paper, seals the flap, and holds it out to me. "Keep this with you," he says.

"What is it?" I ask.

"My name."

"What do I want with your name all shut away in a sealed envelope?"

"You don't but you might, tomorrow or a hundred tomorrows from now." I can't object to his poetic speech. It goes with him.

"But why give it to me?"

The Hunter seems submerged, for several lengthening seconds, in his thoughts. Then his head lifts even higher and he walks to the doorway. He turns but I only get a three-quarter view. The rest is toward the mountains, framing him with the violet of the evening sky and the charcoal outlines of the pine trees.

"Because you might need it," he replies very low in his chest.

Before I can respond he is gone and I am left, the envelope in my hand, in such a wilderness of puzzlement that I plunge out into the twigs and briars of the pathway and welcome the small hurts of the branches and thorns switching at my hands and face as I run downward.

I slow as I come to the start of the cobbled streets because my breath is so short it burns my lungs. Why should I care for one-thousandth of a second what this freak of a man thinks about me and my existence? What does he

know, appearing like a black spook twice in my life and assuming his ideas and opinions are the right ones? Let him take his whole nutty self back to wherever he came from and let him stay there forever, and never, never again let his shadow fall across mine! Bewitched, is it? For all I know he may be the Devil himself!

I hunch my body more securely into my coat and wiggle my icy toes inside my still new, unscuffed shoes. I'm me, Gilly Ground, and I live very well and I know where my gratitude goes — right straight in front of me, behind the solid oak front door of Master Kobalt's house. I think, as I enter the cosiness of the heated hall, that I have let the envelope drop into one of my pockets but I don't bother to check. I smell the meaty steam of the soup pot and go upstairs to take off my coat. I look around my room and its comfort and neatness enclose me and sluff off the wildness of the past hour. But some niggly impulse leads me to the drawer where my grandmother's picture lies safe and snug under my shirts and I guess I intend to look at it, but before my hand reaches in to pull it out I slam the drawer tight shut and take to the stairs two at a time.

6

While I am setting out the soup bowls, the wedge of supper cheese, and the bread, I am just as busy rubbing a mental smudge, as I used to do on my arithmetic papers, all over my meeting with the Hunter. I don't want any permanent design left in my memory of his face, his words, or even the tower, so lovely and lonely, blued by the dusk.

I lift up the lid of the pot and inhale the odor of the thick soup that is our daily dinner and this helps me to meld back into my frame of Kobalt's routine. Then I realize something is missing. The dog. He is always at full length under the kitchen table when I come in at six. Maybe he got shut out by mistake, though this would be almost impossibly unlikely.

I call, "Mash! Here, Mash!" but no click, click of his ungainly paws across the slick floor. And as I involuntarily look at their absence I see something that sends me cold with shock: a trail of dark drops streak the surface of the stone.

I lower the fire under the soup, straighten the spoons that have been joggled sideways by my colliding with the table as I spy the stains, and then, with a half-hour to go before Kobalt will leave his work for the day, I follow the scarlet track. My alarm mounts as the droplets become blobs and then splashes, but at last they cease in front of the tool shed in the corner of the rose garden. I rip open the door and then I am down on my knees beside the shuddering, no longer mud-colored heap of dog. I grab up a sack from the corner, gather him into my arms, and stagger back to the kitchen. I drop the burlap on the floor, nudge it flat with one toe, and lay him as gently as I can on top of it. I reach for the dish towel but my hand stops in midair as though controlled by an invisible force. It digs into my pocket and draws out a handkerchief. I am talking in a whisper to Mash while I drench the cloth in running water and then begin to wipe him clean of clots and dried stripes of blood. The dog never whimpers or moves as time after time I squeeze out the handkerchief and return to bathe his wounds. I don't know what I am saying to him, I just let any old thing rise into my mouth and come out, but somewhere I think I tell him a piece of a fairy tale about a prince who was changed into a beast. It is the first story I remember being told by someone who must have been my grandmother. I am hurrying to get done before Kobalt's entrance but I keep on pretending my fingers are really feathers so I won't hurt the dog. I see that the slashes are not deep and that there will be no scars. The bleeding has stopped. He must have been whipped early, maybe before I left my room for the mountains. I remind myself like a litany behind my murmuring to Mash that he is Kobalt's dog, not mine, and the "not mine, not mine" musics itself into a tune that sounds like the moans of wind around the broken window-hole of my tower. Now he has raised his head and is staring at me with the same muddy eyes I think I saw so long ago this morning in my own mirror. I have finished wiping the last injured inch of him when I hear the pounding tread of Kobalt coming through the hall. I stuff the handkerchief into my pants pocket, prop Mash on his feet and whisk the sacking out of sight into a bottom cupboard, and just as I come out of my stoop, I feel something wet and velvety swipe across the back of my left hand. Only once, one single caress of a lick, from an animal who never before showed any caring. Somehow this injects me with enough strength to show myself as calm as a boulder in a blizzard as Master Kobalt strides in and takes his seat at the table.

I am resolved to do what I do, small as it is, so after I have ladled out the soup and Kobalt is already eating I simply sit there and do not pick up my spoon. It is six mouthfuls before the man notices my stillness. Between dipping in a seventh time and carrying the load of meat chunks and vegetables to his lips he says, "Well? You are sick?"

I try to look into his eyes but they are directed at my bowl. "No," I answer, my voice thready but clear. "Mash is."

The short, giant-muscled carpenter permits what seems like two minutes to be ticked off by the five kitchen clocks. Then he points with his spoon toward the floor. "You have some scrubbing up to do after supper."

The dog is behind my chair. I can hear his breathing. I want to let the whole thing drop into yesterday right then and there but that tiny, tired whuffling of breath keeps me bold.

"Why?" I ask. "Why did you beat him?"

Kobalt's shoulders hoist in what might or what might not be a shrug. "He is getting old. I will soon need another dog and Mash must learn to die."

The words are like a blow on the back of my neck, stunning my body into paralysis. As though the scene were a hundred miles away, I sit there and watch this man finish his soup to the last cube of potato, wipe his broad mouth carefully with his napkin, get up and go into the living room. I go on sitting until I am aware that my stomach juices are slowly rising into my throat. Quickly I get up, the soup bowl clutched in one hand, and place it before Mash. My legs and arms are so weighted I nearly drop the cheese plate as I mechanically replace it in the cooler and the bread I can't swallow seems baked of lead as I put it into its special box. But at last the room is as it was. I feel something warm bump the back of my knees. It is the dog, leaning against me as if to tell me it is okay with him — a "don't worry" kind of pressure. I kneel down beside him and rub my cheek against one of his limp ears.

Am I, too, a dog, a human dog, to be trained and used until I am no longer young or willing enough to co-operate? Am I, too, learning to die? The Hunter's words strike back at me: "Are you bewitched, boy?" and now there is no anger in me but something much worse — fear.

I tiptoe into the hall and see Kobalt in his chair by the fire, reading his book on time patterns, his body as stiffly correct as if he were carved in wood, fastened with concealed glue forever to the silk cushion at his back. I stand, ghostlike, in the dimness as the pages of his book turn to ten, fifteen, twenty — his daily portion of print — and the apprehension seeps out of me. What is there to be afraid of? He is a man, however eccentric, like any other. He sleeps, rises in the morning, eats, works, and draws breath just as I do. If he is also cruel — and I do not forgive the injuries to Mash — then perhaps I, too, have dished out my share of meanness during my less long lifetime, in forms not quite so obvious.

But when he finally resets his book at exact right-angles to the edges of the table beside him, gets up, and goes to his locked room with only a nodded good-night toward me, I'm not so certain why I'm trying to forget the cool horror of his words, "Mash must learn to die."

I squat by the fire and leaf through my memories of my grandmother. She was old, she knew that she had to die, and she never faced anything sideways but lived right up to the last minute and maybe beyond because when they put her in the ground she wasn't in the box. She was behind me where the real things are, like trees and grass and birds in their nests. I never turned to prove her visibility. I didn't have to. Just feeling her presence was enough and I had no tears for the ceremony going on in front of me.

I hang around thinking so long that Mash finally finds sleep in a corner of the hearth without our usual conversation. I am more at home inside myself somehow. Maybe it is the covering warmth of the fire, maybe because my grandmother came close again. But I do know I have to take some kind of action, and what I do is very peculiar.

I sneak into the carpenter shop, change the position of five completed ladders from one wall to another, criss-cross them into a rigid tangle, and then mount quietly to my room. The round, blank moon seems to center my window as though pasted onto the outside of the glass, and I wonder as I take to my bed if my dreams will be sweet or sour.

7

As I am slicing the breakfast bread the next morning I have no chance to rummage through my head to review what my dreaming really was, because suddenly a thundery clatter like nightmare comes from the carpenter shop. It's as though an enormous bird with a wingspread of six feet has got trapped in that large room and is smashing itself against the walls. No such noise — not even a miniature of it — has ever been permitted before in the contrived silence of this house.

I snake through the hall and what I see stops me as short as a wall. Kobalt, his arms flailing, is pushing and

shoving the ladders and lumber into a jumble of giant jackstraws. His lips are drawn back over his stained teeth and his face is as white as glacial snow. Now he begins to kick at the fallen spars of wood as though, at any instant, they might loom upward and strike him down. He seizes a neat stack of finished rungs and hurls them, one by one, at the ceiling. They fall around him like hail, bouncing off his shoulders. What stops this dervish of destruction is the sight of me.

I think he is going to pick me up like a length of wood and smash me against a wall, but instead he freezes into a stillness like the core of a cyclone. His voice is so crowded with growls I have trouble sorting out the words: "It was you! You who moved those ladders! To enrage me. You know what I am and what I wish. Yet you did it, you deliberately did it! You shall be punished, now and —" There he breaks off and a casing of calmness so absolute falls over him I feel the first twinge of real fright. "First you will restore this room to order. Then you are to climb up the tallest ladder and sit there until I tell you to come down. Start now. I am watching."

It takes me what seems a very long time to pick up and restack the havoc of lumber because my hands are awkward with iciness and my arms lack half their power, but at last all is as it was and I obey his final command by humping myself to the summit of the highest jointed ladder in the room and sitting on the top rung. I clench my fingers like clamps to each side of my perch. Is he going to topple it over? Which bones will splinter when I hit the floor?

But he does not approach an inch nearer. Instead he steps into the hall and I hear the lock in the door click it finally shut.

I am not dizzy but I close my eyes. I am attempting to understand. But maybe I really did understand last night when I moved the five ladders from their places. I half-knew what it would do to this strange, time-controlled person who, for some reason I can't discover, gives me good shelter, clothes, food, an opportunity to learn, and a refuge from the disjointed, bonging world of the orphanage. And now I know for sure why I did it. To avenge the whiplashes on the hide of his spiritless dog. And it worked. It bombed him out of his eerie peace. But what happens when the dam cracks or the tree-trunk is sawn through? I wish I could start yesterday over, return to the moment I take the first step up the pathway to the tower and turn about-face, and never go, never meet the Hunter, never be stabbed by the rightness of his question: "Are you bewitched, boy?" If I could magic the fifteen clocks in this house and all the others across the surface of the earth, I would do it.

But I recover no shadow of ease or release from this daydream. It is too fragile. It wisps off the ground glass of what really is, like the cover of morning's first mist. I am a prisoner just as certainly as Kobalt is a prisoner, but the terrible difference is that he chose his dungeon and he has become the jailer of mine.

I shift my weight just enough so as not to shake the ladder. My backbone is aching a little. I force my thoughts to walk forward even if they lead me to a gallows. To him I am a clock to be wound, or a front door to be opened only three times a day, or a creature to make soup and keep the plates clean, or — I halt before the next image but break through its thorns as I used to the thickets on the way to the tower — or a dog. I am no more alive to Kobalt than Mash. And from Mash he drew blood.

I am at the end, the last point of land before drowning, and I clang a steel shutter down over my mind and concentrate on nothingness — a desolate country that shows no green.

I never know the duration of that trancelike session on the ladder and I don't leave the barrenness of the nothing-landscape until I begin to smell the meat for lunch mixing its scent with that of the shaved wood. I open my eyes on Kobalt who fills the threshold with solid sternness. He beckons me down but it is several minutes before I can loosen the tension in my leg and arm joints enough to descend, flat-footed and unsteady.

I think, as I scoop my chair up under the kitchen table and cut into the chunk of beef, that Kobalt will have something to say. If ever, now. But he treats today like all the others with his deep and ordinary habit of silence. I stuff the food into me the way I used to when I was first put into the orphanage, as though the next meal might not show up. Kobalt finishes before me and disappears into his shop. With the torpor of a slug I stack the dishes, wash them, and give them back to their cupboards. I go upstairs, pull out my history book, and fasten myself to the sentence where I left off yesterday. I believe I am reading but I'm not. The page might as well be wiped free of any words at all. I am not in revolutionary France where the book is, but at the window, wondering what is in the locked room neighboring mine, Kobalt's room. I've never really cared before but I do now. It seems important or maybe my newborn curiosity is just an escape from myself. I unlatch the middle frame of the window and push it up. I look down. The high distance from the ground reminds me of those hours on the ladder, though this drop is three times longer, so I twist my head to the right and stare at the protruding window sill of the other room. I note — I have never investigated before — that there is a very narrow ledge running from the base of my sill to his. It would just about support half of my foot if I Indian-walked it.

Suddenly I am invaded by action. I straddle the sill, one leg in, one leg out, shift my weight and, my palms flat against the smooth outer stone, I inch my body across the three feet separating the two windows. I grab hold

of the small jut in the center of Kobalt's window frame, crooking my fingers as tight as I can along the tiny hold, and peer in. I think I get just one blink, one flash of that interior, for in the next instant I am teetering wildly, one foot in midair, and then I fall crashingly downward and land in a crumple on the dirt-packed, grassless ground.

I draw in a couple of breaths to test my ribs. Then I untangle myself and lie spread-eagled, cautiously lifting first my arms, then my legs. Everything works except my left ankle. It seems to be invaded by a porcupine, so full of stings and jabs I stuff my knuckles into my mouth. I force myself into a sitting position. I must get up. After what I saw in that room I know that if I am disabled I am licked, done for. I raise my back upwards with my good leg, using my arms as props, and turn to stand. I make it but even this lightest of pressures on my ankle makes my lunch surge into my throat. I swallow down the bitterness again and again until I can control the convulsions in my stomach. I set my teeth and somehow drag myself into the kitchen. I go down on my knees, crawl to the closet where the cleaning things are stowed, and yank out a long dustcloth. I tear it into three strips and bind them, one after the other, around my ankle which now hurts so piercingly part of me wishes the foot would just drop off.

I use the table to hoist myself erect. I must get back to my room. Kobalt mustn't guess that I am crippled. I hobble as far as the stairs, then seat myself on the first step and with my good leg as a lever begin the tortured, backward journey up that endless flight. I bruise my back each time I slide myself onto the next ledge but I don't care. All that counts is my final arrival in my own room.

At last there are no more steps. Once more I go on all fours and, covering the brief space of hall, collapse into my room, pushing the door closed with my left arm.

I think I lie prone on the floor for a while, because it is not so difficult later to get onto my chair. Now I am once again where I was, facing my history book, but what has gone between, what I have seen, is so bursting with dread I have to fight my own will to make my hand pick up a pencil and draw on a square of paper what I glimpsed in that locked room. I have to redesign it this very instant or I will never believe it exists. My hand jerks and the lines wobble but I keep going, and when I am done I stare at the crude unreality of the sketch until I am certain it is true. It shows a cage made of discarded ladder rungs and side rails. A large cage but not large enough for Kobalt. It is just my size!

I snatch up the sheet of paper, scrabble it into a ball, and then tear it into such minute bits it snows itself all over my blotter.

8

By four o'clock there are no longer six penknives whittling away at my foot. The pain is more of a pound, dull and regular and weakening. I manage the stairs, feeling ashen and very small, and, loaded with the broom, the sweeper, and two dustcloths, I limp into the living room to start my daily cleaning. I have to keep up the appearance of normalcy. I know this as certainly as I know my grandmother loved me. I've learned what happens to Kobalt when the pattern is broken and I can't take any more chances, handicapped as I am with a bum foot.

I wipe off the table tops, skipping the legs for once,

whisk up the possibility of dust from the flooring around the central rug, and have begun to push the sweeper back and forth over the red carpet when, like a faulty clock, I run down to a standstill, lean on the handle for a crutch, and with my free hand scrub off the tears that are slowly runneling down my cheeks. I hate myself. I am not the crying type. This little drift of anger burns off the drip but I can't make my lumpy leg follow the other to complete the expanse of ruddy wool. I have never realized before that Kobalt, closed in his workroom, listens to my movements, but he does, for not two minutes later he comes out and confronts me.

"If you are done in here, why isn't the soup started?" he says, his tufts of eyebrows raised to unhood his round black eyes.

I am stuck. If I walk toward the kitchen he will see the limp. I have to admit something. "I twisted my ankle."

I don't expect what I next see on this broad face. It is a smile. The man is pleased!

"Then I will prepare the vegetables while you clean the silver," he says and stalks into the kitchen. But as he goes I catch the tail-end of a mutter and the words sound like "— won't have to lock the house until night." The first bolt of my imprisonment has been fastened. I can hear its metallic rasp in my mind as clearly as if it had been secured.

Then I connect again with the other living being in this

house — Mash. The discovery of the cage, the accident, and the pain had thrust him out of my thoughts until this moment when I follow the Master into the kitchen. Where is he? His usual corners are vacant of him. He has not been present since last night. Even his cage, that small replica of what is upstairs, is gone.

Kobalt has already set out the huge box of knives and forks and spoons with the silver polish and rags beside it. I sit in the chair to ease the throb in my left leg but before I pick up the first fork I speak. "What has happened to the dog?"

The answer comes from his back. "I put him out."

For some reason I don't believe him. Maybe because his voice is full of the same strangeness as the smile he gives me when I tell him I am hurt.

I half rise up.

"Get at that silver!" This is an order I dare not challenge, not now that I have lost the advantage of swiftness, which is all I have against his bulging strength.

I duck my head and dip the rag into the bottle of polish and as I meticulously rub at the pure shining of the untarnished surfaces I summon up my full stock of patience, waiting for the clocks to strike five, when my free hour is due.

Somehow I manage to clink the last spoon back into the box by the second chiming of the clock chorus and, Kobalt tucked away in his workroom as always, I head for the back door. I anticipate the sight of Mash's lank longness against the rosebushes, his misshapen head alerting to my coming and maybe even one of those quivers of his tail that no one but me recognizes as a wag. I want him to be there so much that for an instant I imagine him out of thin air, but it is only a clump of wintering grass. Hastily I scan the entire area of the garden. He is nowhere. I limp across to the tool shed and open the door. The pitchfork and shovel glint back at me in the westering light of new evening. Some kind of cold is getting at me, though the night frost is still far off and no wind touches the leaves of the roses.

Then my mounting fear is answered. In one corner of the tiny shed is a pile of sticks, particular sticks that once were something else. Each one has been snapped in half and the sight of their raw, splintered ends pierces my insides with anguish. It is the wreckage of Mash's cage. Oh, my dear dog! For the first time in over a year, that long-ago morning when my grandmother's hut was locked against me forever, I want to open my mouth and roar, let out a shout that will shake the mountains, uproot a whole forest of trees, echo and re-echo for twenty hours, bashing itself from one crag to another like a condor gone crazy. But the yell is never birthed. Instead my jaws close so tight together my teeth hurt. I stand there as fixed as a lance driven deep into the earth and try to spirit myself back into the orphanage, back before Kobalt, before the carpeted, cushioned, and dreadful cosiness of his house. I re-create the shattering bonging of the orphanage bells, the grey taste of the gruelly meals, the exhausting hours at the woodpile where my wrists, bared by sleeves too short for my arms, were banded by steel strips of cold. But at last the surf of my retreat from the present hurls me back and I hear again Mrs. Heister's voice telling me that if I fail with Master Kobalt I shall be sent to the city institution for the homeless where my future will be meager and miserable. I cannot return to what was, not ever.

I stump into the house. I know without knowing that my hour is over. I go to the kitchen and when I see the ladder maker giving the soup a final stir before pouring it into the two bowls on the counter, just as he has done day after day and as he will do until I will no longer even be able to count them, my jaws loosen and an involuntary sound issues from my mouth, half groan, half hiccough.

He turns. "Perhaps you are not fit to be up," he says and there is a kind of subterranean relish behind the words.

My insides leap alive. I shovel my grief for Mash under as many layers of consciousness as I can. I recognize the danger now and it is as keen-edged as the blade that kills.

I answer quickly, "Oh, no. I'm fine." I force my lame foot to take its full share of my weight as I walk to the table and fight to keep my face from revealing what this costs. As clearly as if a guillotine had suddenly replaced the innocence of the table set for supper, I know what waits for me upstairs the very moment I am no longer of use to this madman. I am as expendable as the dog. But what booms in my mind louder than any bell anywhere, with an insistence that even cuts through the horror of this truth, is the knowing that I must escape even if I die in the doing.

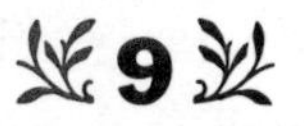

The soup I sit down to tastes like clay but I funnel it in for the future. The meals to come might be roots and berries if the tower is to become my refuge until my ankle heals. Or food scraps, shoved through the wooden bars of that insane cell waiting in Kobalt's room. Or maybe just plain nothing at all until I dwindle to a size for convenient burial.

I finally achieve the bottom of the bowl and Kobalt motions for me to clear the table. I feel his gaze encircle me like a thong so taut it burns the skin and this helps me not to totter as each step rivers my bad leg with pain. I get everything stacked and am about to sit down anywhere when the man says, "This time you may wash up now instead of tomorrow. You skimped your duties before supper."

This acts on me like an announcement of change, a kind of declaration that tomorrow will be different, disastrously different. I have tonight and that's all. Kobalt waits until the faucet is gushing hot water into the dishpan and then he takes himself, as usual, into the living room to his single book.

My mind is so absent from my actions that I accidentally nick my thumb with the cheese knife. A tiny rivulet of blood swirls into the froth of soap and I am filled with the thought of Mash. Are there such things as ghost dogs? And is his wraith, now blanched to white, prowling the outside of the house, moaning softly in its lostness? I tell myself not to be an idiot but my body continues to act like one, gripped in a cadence of minor shivers.

The dishes done, I pack a sack with bread and cheese and stash it under a small chair in the hall. I recline awkwardly on the staircase, beginning the long watch that will end with Kobalt closing his book and going to bed. In spite of my awareness of how I am islanded by complete peril, I drowse, jerk awake, and drowse again.

By some flick of fortune I hear a shrill squeak of metal on metal and come wholly up out of the furry temptation of sleep. I see Kobalt fastening the padlocks on the windows and realize he must have thus sealed the entire house. And with the keys in his pocket and himself finally locked into his bedroom there will be no exit for me. Not unless I can somehow devise one.

He passes me on the stairs without a sign and clomps out of hearing. I take my place by the low-burning fire but all my former delight in the kingdom of illumined charcoal and chips has vanished. Now the redness reminds me of my missing companion who used to listen to my talking with his head lovingly cocked as though he understood. The warmth does not penetrate the rising sense of danger within me but, rather, seems to scorch. I fish around in my head for a way out. If I break a pane of glass, chances are Kobalt will hear it. He is not such a fool as not to guess I might try to run off. Prying up one of the window locks is impossible. I haven't the right tools. I consider using Mash's rope to lower myself out of my window but my room is too close to Kobalt's. Short of burning down the house I can't see a way and I'm not up to committing arson. Besides, only the interior would catch and the smoke would set an alarm before any outlet broke through.

Then I think of the workroom, what fills it, and the fireplace. Maybe, just maybe, I could do it! I creep into the shop, propping the door wide open with a wedge of wood, grab up a coil of rope, and with the quiet of a cat I lower that tallest, joined ladder sideways and carry it soundlessly into the living room. Now I must extinguish the fire first but I don't dare get water from the kitchen. The gurgle of the pipes would betray me. I lift up a large hunk of the carpet and throw it onto the embers, then beat it with the flats of my hands until I am certain not even a spark is left alive. I haul back the smoldering rug and start the narrow ladder on its upward journey, length by length, into the chimney. It is an inch-by-inch voyage and even at that the side rails scrape three or four times on the bricks. Each time I pause and listen but there is no hint of a stir upstairs.

At last it rests steadily on its legs. I retrieve the sack of food and loop its end twice around my belt. Then I take a deep breath and begin the ascent. At the fifth rung my bum ankle starts to resent the strain so violently I have to halt until the worst of the pain lessens. The wide shaft of brick shows a star at the end of it, and as I hoist myself up and up again I pretend that's why I am climbing. I will pocket it and save its small shining all the rest of my life to remember my grandmother by. I have had to leave her photograph and this is making me sad. It's all I have from our years together, except the one thing she could afford to give generously—her love. I don't laugh at myself for this childish fantasy about the star because I need it to get me out. Twice I smother sneezes. The lining of the chimney is coated with soot that furs into my nose and mouth.

When my head finally pops out into the lighter darkness of the night I wave to the star for helping me and with my arms pull my body up and over the edge like a cork. Before the wedge of a doubt can call me a coward, I tie one end of the rope around the chimney and secure it with a good knot. I lower the other end down the side of the house opposite Kobalt's room. Then, grasping the rope with both hands, I lie down on the slate tiles and slide, monkey-fashion, foot by foot, down the slant until I reach the overhang. So far there has been no sound but the chitter of an awakened bird somewhere among the roses.

I scoop myself over the edge of the roof, and for an instant, as I dangle with only my hands to hold me aloft, I want to let go, to stop trying and find at the bottom of the drop the kind of peace given to my grandmother and Mash. I'm suddenly no bigger to myself than a flea on the hide of an elephant, with a very good chance of being crushed, either right now or later. I think what arrests me is the second series of chirps from that bird in the garden. It's as though he were calling me down.

Hand over hand I swing quickly to the ground, landing safely on my good leg. I listen intently. Even the bird is still. I bend to tighten the outer binding around my ankle and then slowly, like a crooked stick, I leave the garden and start the cobbled way up the street.

I try to choose the smoothest stones for my injured foot but more often than not my shoe slips and the tendons wrench. To shut out part of the agony, I begin to plan my next move. First the tower. I have to hole up for at least a couple of days to give my ankle a rest before I take the long trip to the city. Maybe I'll be picked up on the highway and jailed as a vagrant. Maybe I'll end up, as Mrs. Heister said I would, in the institution where they care even less than she did about people with no homes. Maybe I'll become a nasty little squinched-up, squeezed-dry nobody, bitter as a lemon and no good to anybody. I saw a couple of these in the orphanage but I never looked twice. They were vanquished kids who never said no to anything. Maybe. But I'm still me, Gilly Ground, and I'm about to fight for my freedom even if my kind offers me nothing better than hunger cramps and colds in the head. I'm not courageous. I haven't any other choice.

This effort takes me onto the trail and now the night voices close in. At first I say to myself, "That's just an owl" — "Okay, so a weasel is out hunting," but gradually the paddings and cracklings and sighings move over the boundary of reality and get ghosty. Maybe it's because I'm tired, so blasted tired I let a log take a sock at my leg rather than go around it, but the pines are haunted for me now and my common sense recedes into a faraway country where shadows are giants and the tree branch ahead is a faceless monster with claws six inches long. I think I scream once when I lurch into a thicket that seems to clutch me all over trying to drag me down. I tear myself

free and jam my hands into my pockets to give the Things less to grab at.

And that's when I find it — the little square shape of an envelope entrenched at the bottom of my pants pocket. The ghouls retreat as the tall form of the Hunter fills my memory. I've got a place to go if I can make it!

I stumble into the tower and, falling to the floor, throw my elbows onto the seat of the throne I built so long, long ago and place my head in the aching anchorage of my arms.

When I can, when it is easier to straighten my back and lift my head, I look around at the high, weather-broken place that was my joy and my home. I try to recover the truth it once was to me, a round barricade to hold the sunlight, the armored thoughts of knights and quests and nobility to come. But I can't go back. What I see now — that almost black darkness layering spiders' webs and hidden lizards and the delicate flutterings of bats — cancels the way it was like a splotch of dirty ink across the illuminated page of a fairy tale.

Maybe a mouthful of cheese and bread would drive down this new misery to where I wouldn't have to face it. I fumble for the sack I stole from the kitchen. It isn't there. I have dropped it on the way. So I sit there and let my tower soundlessly tumble around me. It is no more of a shelter than my anonymous cot among twenty others at the orphanage. It is as roofless and doorless and chill as I am. It once belonged to someone who was a child, a person who carried hope like a shield and eagerness like a sword. Now it is itself, bare and ruined and useless. And I am myself, a thin and bony container for hunger and thirst and inner frost.

I sit there on the dream-forsaken stones and watch the sky pale into the whitish green of just before dawn and when I hear it coming — the final horror stomping up the path — I am not surprised and I do not move. I listen but I cannot care.

The yelling starts two hundred yards below the tower. "Come out, boy! Come out!" No beast ever scraped his gullet raw with such roaring. "I know you are there! I found your tracks!"

I get to my feet and look from the slit of a window. The squat, invincible hulk that is Kobalt is waving its arms wildly. The sack of food flies into the air from his left hand like the body of a small animal and smashes against the trunk of a tree. And in his right is the uplifted shape of an iron-headed hammer as large as an axe.

"Come out! I order you out!" he shouts. "If I can't have you the way I want you I'll have you dead!"

10

It is now. I know it is now. I can stand still in my nothingness and be murdered or I can fight for my life. I am suddenly free, free of the orphanage, the bondage of Kobalt, free even of myself. I don't decide. I don't even think. I move.

I pick up a handful of stones and shower them at the enemy. One of them gets his shoulder. He grunts and halts his advance. "That will do you no good!" he yells, though he is so near I would hear him whisper. "I will have you under the earth sooner or later!"

I use these seconds to rearm. The next hail of rocks I

aim higher and two small ones bounce off his forehead.

He raises his hammer to the sky, whirling it like a sling. If I can de-weapon him I've got a better chance, not much but better. "Throw it!" I call out. "Go on, get me!" I step into the entrance of the tower in full view.

The man tilts his massive head backwards and booms into hideous laughter. "I'm not that stupid, my little cock! Crow on! I'll snap you off at the neck by sunup!"

He blocks me like an oak, so solid, so strong he might be rooted. I realize my sole hope is to get past him somehow, dodge the slaughtering swipe of that deadly hammer, and, because I can't run, roll down the mountain to get a head start on his pursuit. I have to show myself, come all the way into the open. I know it may be a fool's move but it is the only one I have. The tower has become a trap.

I feel one stroke of the rising sun like a last blessing on my cheeks as I come forward — a final touch of life. A blur of wood and iron swishes past my left ear as I duck and try to swerve out of range. I stumble and go down on my knees.

"I've got you now!" screeches the madman. He lunges in for the kill.

I hug my arms around me tight like I used to my grandmother when the dark had almost conquered me. I wait for death.

But suddenly I am still here and Kobalt is enwrapped

in a fury of snarls and snaps and mud-colored fur! Blood streaks the man's neck and something as savage as a bull-whip is tearing at his right arm. The hammer careens down the hill and Kobalt is thrashing in all directions trying to throw off this ferocious hound of hell. It is Mash!

The man leaps backward, trips, and crashes onto his spine. The dog covers him from knee to neck, teeth bared and about to clench into his flesh. But Kobalt is still, as still as the boulder under his head.

I throw myself onto the dog and pull him off. I hang on until the shudders leave his bony frame and his heaving breath quiets to quick panting. I loosen my hold and he turns his eyes to mine and licks my face.

"That's enough," I sort of croon in his lank ear. "He is alive. Leave him that way. It's better for both of us."

Mash tells me he understands and consents with his now truly wagging tail. Then he wiggles himself free of me and dives into a nearby bush. I believe for an instant that he is abandoning his rescue and I know I won't make it down the mountain and to the city without him. But there he is again and he has retrieved the broken sack of food. He lays it at my feet and looks at me, his tongue lolling sideways in what must be his first grin.

The sun is real now, the mountains true, the pine trees restored to the horizon. And Mash and me, we're hungry.

I thank him for the food and get up. "We must go

now, no matter if we can hardly walk," I say to him, to my beautiful hero-dog. "We'll eat on the way."

I think I must be smiling, because his tail takes up its newly learned rhythm of joy. We have troubles getting ourselves down that uneven, thickety path because when I fell under the hammer my ankle got another twist. But the pain is only pain and I have someone to help me with his love. Mash doesn't yet know how to frisk but he's coming close in his own gallumping way.

Anyway, it isn't important how we finally arrive at and pass through the village. We do it, together. It is still early and the streets are bare of people. I pause only once, in front of the square stone house. I speak to my friend. "No one will ever know any of this," I say, "except you and me. Kobalt will go on getting richer in ladders and poorer in time."

Then I know there is one more thing I have to do before I leave my past forever. I find a sharp-edged pebble, I lift my hand to the door, and I scratch into the slick varnished wood, wide and free, two words, my last message to the false and captive world I once desired. I have to. It is an ending before my beginning. And I never know, until Mash and I long later belong and are a family to the Hunter, and I am sent to school where I want to shine as bright as I really am, that one of these two last words is misspelled.

"DORP DEAD!"

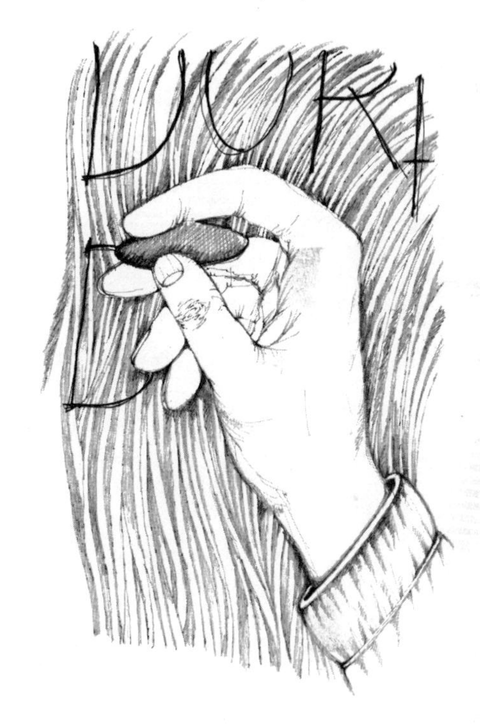

About the Author

Julia Cunningham, author of *Macaroon* and *Candle Tales,* attended a variety of schools, but considers herself self-educated. Although there was a time when she hoped to be a painter or a musician, she has found that words suit her best. Miss Cunningham has lived in New York City and France, and now is settled in Santa Barbara, California, where she is a bookseller when she is not writing.